Scholastic Children's Books,
Euston House, 24 Eversholt Street,
London NW1 1DB, UK

A division of Scholastic Ltd
London ~ New York ~ Toronto ~ Sydney ~ Auckland
Mexico City ~ New Delhi ~ Hong Kong

First published in the US by Penguin Random House, 2017
First published in the UK by Scholastic Ltd, 2017

ISBN 978 1407 17141 8

Printed and bound in the UK by CPI Group (UK) Ltd, Croydon CR0 4YY

2 4 6 8 10 9 7 5 3 1

www.scholastic.co.uk

DREAMWORKS

Trolls
Holiday

ADAPTED BY DAVE LEWMAN

SCHOLASTIC

CHAPTER
1

Early one bright and sunny morning, Poppy proclaimed from the big stage in the centre of Troll Village with her arms spread wide, "I hereby announce that Super-Scrapbooking Day is OFFICIALLY OPEN!"

"Hurray for our awesome Queen Poppy!" the Trolls cheered. "We love Super-Scrapbooking Day!"

BOOM! Cannons fired clouds of sparkling glitter into the air! Thumping music got everyone moving and grooving, dancing and scrapbooking!

Another celebration had begun in Troll Village.

The Trolls loved holidays, so they had lots and lots of them. Practically every day of the year, they celebrated a special holiday. Super-Scrapbooking Day was a particular favourite of Poppy's, since she adored scrapbooking. The whole day was dedicated to the tools and materials that made scrapbooking possible. Scissors! Felt! Glue! Glitter! Scraps! Pictures! Drawings!

Super-Scrapbooking Day was jam-packed with fun activities. Harper, who loved art, showed the Trolls how to make their scrapbooks more artistic. King Peppy told young Trolls thrilling stories about the adventures of scrapbooking heroes in the olden days. Guy Diamond showed everyone how to dance new steps while they added the sparkle of glitter to their creations.

"Now move your legs like they're a pair of scissors!" Guy called out in his shimmery voice as he demonstrated the move. "Yeah! That's it! Cut and cut and snip and snip. Now ... *glitter!*"

In the afternoon, there was a scrapbook parade with Trolls dressed up as bottles of glue and glitter. The tallest Troll, Biggie, wore a costume that made him look like a giant walking scrapbook. Biggie marched proudly through the village square carrying his pet worm, Mr Dinkles, who was wearing a matching costume.

"Oh, Mr Dinkles!" Biggie cried as he waved to his friends. "This year's parade is even more fun than last year's!"

"Mew!" said Mr Dinkles.

Everyone had put their best scrapbooks on display for all to admire. Judges strolled past, peering at the Trolls' work and awarding prizes. Prettiest Scrapbook! Scrappiest Scrapbook! Glitteriest Scrapbook! Biggest Scrapbook! Tiniest

Scrapbook! On Super-Scrapbooking Day, everyone was a winner.

While wandering around the village admiring the beautiful scrapbooks, Poppy spotted Branch working hard on a scrapbook of his own.

"Branch!" she said, surprised. "You're making a scrapbook? I thought you were against scrapbooking!"

Branch looked up, happy to see her. "I never said that!" he insisted. "I mean, maybe once or twice you kind of drove me a little bit crazy with all your scrapbooking, but I never said I was against it."

"All right! Good for you!" Poppy said. "May I see your scrapbook?"

Branch hastily hid it behind his back. "It's not done," he said. "I'm not really ready to show it to anyone yet. It's actually my first scrapbook ever."

"Aw, c'mon!" Poppy said, grinning. "Gimme a sneak peek!"

4

"Well…" Branch said, hesitating, "okay. But promise you won't laugh!" He slowly brought the small scrapbook out from behind his back.

"I won't laugh – no way! What's the theme of your scrapbook?" Poppy asked eagerly. "Rainbows? Cupcakes? Oooh, I know! Rainbows made out of cupcakes!"

Branch rolled his eyes. "Rainbows made out of cupcakes? How is that even possible?"

"With scrapbooking, ANYTHING is possible!" Poppy enthused. "So what's your theme?"

"Rocks."

"*Rocks?*"

"Yeah. Rocks."

Poppy looked confused. She'd seen scrapbooks dedicated to all kinds of things – birthdays, fashion shows, mushrooms, pets – but not rocks. She'd never even *heard* of a scrapbook about rocks. And

she wasn't sure why anyone would want to make one. But Branch was her friend, so she was willing to give rocks a chance.

"Okay," she said slowly, "Bring on the rocks!"

Branch flipped through the thick pages of his scrapbook, showing Poppy what he'd done so far. Most of the pages featured lumpy grey rocks made of felt.

"I think rocks are great!" he said. "You might even say that rocks rock!" He waited a moment for Poppy to laugh at his little joke. She didn't. "Or you might not." He frowned slightly.

"I guess rocks are pretty cool," Poppy said. "Kind of. I guess ... um ... like when you stub your toe on one and the fuzzy rock-felt squishes up between your toes and makes you giggle."

"Rocks are great for all kinds of reasons," Branch said. "You can build a house with rocks.

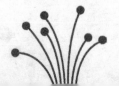

You can make a firepit with rocks. You can hold things down so they don't blow away…"

"You can skip rocks across water," Poppy suggested.

"Really?" Branch asked. "Are you sure? Seems like they'd sink."

Poppy touched one of the rocks in Branch's book.

"Well, I think your scrapbook's great!" she said.

"You do?" Branch said, pleased. "Thanks!"

"Just one small suggestion?"

"What?"

She looked around to see if anyone was listening. "More glitter," she whispered.

"I don't know," Branch said, rubbing his chin. "Most rocks aren't very glittery."

"But *some* are," Poppy said. "And in my experience, you can never have too much glitter! Especially on Super-Scrapbooking Day!"

With Branch participating, the holiday was an especially great success. The Trolls finished off with a big bonfire, lots of cookies shaped like scrapbooks, and a special oversized scrapbook they made together to help them remember the day. They went to bed happy that night, even if they were worn out from all the scrapbooking, partying, dancing and singing. But they had to rest up and get their strength back quickly, because New Hair's Eve was just around the corner!

Meanwhile, in Bergen Town, nobody had celebrated Super-Scrapbooking Day. It wasn't a Bergen holiday. As a matter of fact, *no* day was a Bergen holiday any more.

In the past, the Bergens had one big holiday: Trollstice. But they'd cancelled it for ever when they became friends with the Trolls, as Trollstice had unfortunately involved the eating of Trolls. Poppy and Bridget had shown the Bergens that being *friends* with Trolls made them happier than they'd feel *eating* them. And as King Gristle had said when he'd announced the permanent cancellation of Trollstice, "You can't be friends with someone and eat them, too."

Not that the Bergens never had fun nowadays. They weren't nearly as miserable as they'd been before the Trolls had helped them find the happiness inside themselves. They were perfectly capable of being happy. They just weren't very *good* at it.

One Bergen's idea of fun was to organize a picnic at a mud puddle. Nobody came. In fact, even the Bergen who'd invited everyone to the picnic didn't show up.

Another Bergen thought it might be fun to play

football with a wooden cube. She ended up in the hospital.

One little Bergen discovered that when he hit an empty log with a stick, it made a nice sound. *THWACK! THWACK! THWACK!* He tried to make up a happy song to go with the thwacking, but then the stick broke.

Some Bergens invented a board game called Roll the Die and Move Your Piece Around the Square. But it wasn't much fun, even if you won – which was hard to determine anyway.

None of these things seemed worth celebrating as a special holiday.

So while the Trolls were having a wonderful time on Super-Scrapbooking Day, the Bergens had simply gone about their usual business, doing chores and the like, not anything particularly special.

But what about Gristle, the king of the Bergens,

and Bridget, his true love? What were those two lovebirds up to? Were they happy? Excited? Joyful? Thrilled?

CHAPTER 2

Actually … they were bored.

"Boring! Boring!" cawed a big black Cawkoo
outside a castle window. It fluffed up its black
feathers and peeked in to see if anyone was listening.
They weren't.

Inside, King Gristle and Bridget slouched on two
thrones set up next to each other in the throne room.
By the room's dim light, Bridget read a copy of *Bergen
Beat* magazine. She wore a small crown, a royal robe
with a white fur collar and a jewelled clasp and pink
slippers. Gristle had a little keyboard on his lap. He

was trying to play "Chopsticks", but he couldn't get past the first part without making a mistake.

Gristle looked over at Bridget. "Anything interesting in your magazine?"

"Not really," she said, listlessly turning the pages. "Having fun with your keyboard?"

"I think maybe it's broken," he answered. "It keeps making mistakes."

Bridget yawned. King Gristle started to slowly pick out the notes to "Chopsticks" again.

A few more dull days went by...

In Troll Village, Cooper walked around on his four Troll legs (twice the usual number for a Troll), collecting mail.

"Mail!" he called cheerfully. "Bring out your mail!"

After he'd gathered it all, he quickly delivered it.

This was easy, since most of the time he only had to walk over to the next pod and hand its owner a card or a party invitation. "Here's your mail!" he'd say cheerfully. "Enjoy!"

But today's batch of mail had an envelope addressed to "King Gristle and Bridget, The Castle, Bergen Town".

"Bergen Town!" Cooper exclaimed. "Time to use the Zip Beetle Express!"

Now that the Trolls and the Bergens were friends, they occasionally sent messages back and forth. It was a long way from Troll Village to Bergen Town (especially for a Troll), but luckily some Zip Beetles were happy to help out. They loved nothing better than running, so if a Troll wanted to send a message to a Bergen, he or she had only to ask a Zip Beetle to carry it there.

Cooper headed to the edge of Troll Village and

shouted into the forest, "Zip Beetle Express, please!"

In no time at all, a Zip Beetle appeared and took the envelope from him. Before Cooper could thank the critter, it had zipped off into the woods towards Bergen Town. When he started to slow down a tiny bit, another Zip Beetle took the envelope from him and zoomed away on its fresh, rested legs. After passing from critter to critter, the card reached the Bergen Town Post Office in record time!

Unfortunately, the Bergen in charge of delivering mail was not speedy at all. When the Zip Beetle arrived with the envelope, the postman roused himself from a soothing nap, stretched and ambled across the room to the waiting critter.

But when he saw who the envelope was addressed to, the carrier's manner changed instantly.

"King Gristle!" he yelped. "Gotta go!" He ran all the way to the castle as fast as his stiff Bergen legs could carry him, at one point leaping over a mud puddle where no one was having a picnic. (Well, the Bergens never had picnics there.) Exhausted, he handed the envelope to one of the tall guards at the front gate.

"For the king!" he said, gasping for breath.

"Yeah, I figured," the guard said. "Since you were running. For once."

Inside the castle, King Gristle and Bridget were still sitting on their thrones. They'd tried trading seats, but then determined that it didn't make a difference.

BOOM! The big wooden doors to the throne room swung open and hit the walls. An old family painting fell to the floor. *CRASH!*

Gristle jumped. "How many times have I told you not to slam those doors?" he complained. "We really should install doorstops. The walls are getting all marked up."

Two guards strode across the vast room, their

heavy steps echoing off the walls. One of the guards carried the envelope, which was covered in stars, rainbows, stickers and glitter. Glitter stuck to the guard's hand and fluttered to the floor.

"Got another card from Troll Village," he announced, handing it to King Gristle with a respectful bow.

"Oooh, yay!" Bridget cooed, leaning over to peek. "A card!"

"Thanks, Todd," King Gristle said.

"I'm Chad," the guard said. He pointed a thumb towards the other guard. "He's Todd."

Todd waved at the king. "Hi," he said sheepishly. Since he and Chad were identical twins dressed in identical uniforms, it was very difficult to tell them apart.

But King Gristle kept trying. "Yup, got it. Chod and Tadd."

The guards shrugged and didn't correct him. After all, he was the king.

Bridget pointed at the sparkly envelope. "Oooh look, Grissy," she said happily. "It's another holiday card from my friend Poppy!"

Gristle peered at the card, reading the message inside. "'Happy Catch Your Friend Day'? What if you drop her? I mean, we're not insured for that kind of thing."

"Oh, I would never, ever drop Poppy," Bridget said, placing the card on the fireplace mantel next to the dozens of other holiday cards from her Troll friend. "Never."

"Whatevs, babe," King Gristle replied, shrugging. "The Trolls have so many holidays! *Too* many, if you ask me." He walked over to the mantel and picked up a card at random. "Look at this one. It says 'Happy Happy Holidays Day!' For reals? Not

for me. I mean, come on!"

"Well, I think it's kind of nice," Bridget said, "having so much to celebrate." She looked sadly at all the cards.

Gristle saw that Bridget looked unhappy, so he tried to cheer her up.

"Hey, Bridgie – we do cool stuff, too! I mean, what about all the awesome cards we've sent back to the Trolls? Huh?"

At that very moment in Troll Village, Cooper was delivering a card from the Bergens to Poppy. Poppy eagerly tore open the plain brown envelope and looked at the card. She saw an awkward picture of Bridget and Gristle. The king held a handwritten sign that said MONDAY.

"'Monday'," Poppy read. "Well, that's … consistent." She placed the card on the fuzzy wall of her pod next to several others like it. All the Trolls had pictures of Gristle and Bridget holding up signs with the days of the week written on them. "Branch … Bridget, um, sent another card…"

She turned and saw Branch looking at himself in her mirror. He was making a face that looked tense. Painful, even.

"What are you doing?" Poppy asked. "What's happening with your face? Are you about to barf? I'll go get a dustbin…"

Branch shook his head. "No, I'm practising my smile." He saw his friend looking confused and tried to explain. "You know, I'm new to this whole being happy thing."

He tried again, stretching his lips open tightly. It didn't look like a smile. More like a grimace. Or like he was about to bite someone. Poppy winced.

"Oh! Well, here – let me help," she offered.

"Smiles are my thing!"

"No, that's okay. I can—" Branch protested.

But Poppy put her hands on his face, trying to show him the right way to smile. She pushed up the corners of his mouth. "Hmm … nope." She pulled up his cheeks. "Gettin' there … almost!" She pushed and pulled, moving the blue skin on his face around. "Cute, but not quite. Weird. Your face is being very frustrating."

Branch pulled away, shook his face and tried to change the subject back to the greeting cards from the Bergens. He walked over to the wall and studied the dull cards Poppy had pinned up.

"What is the deal with all these?" he asked. "'Monday'. 'Friday'. 'Sunday, Mid-Morning'?"

Poppy shrugged. "It's like ever since Trollstice was cancelled, the Bergens don't have anything to look forward to! I feel really bad for them."

Poppy thought about the Bergens having nothing to look forward to, and it made her very sad – especially when she thought about her best friend, Bridget, never getting to celebrate a wonderful, fun holiday. She just had to do something for her bestie Bridget.

Then, as if an explosion of colourful jelly beans and sparkling glitter had gone off in her head, Poppy got a GREAT, BIG, EXCITING IDEA!

CHAPTER
3

Branch saw the ecstatic look on Poppy's face and instantly grew alarmed.

"No, no, no!" he protested, holding both hands up. "I know what that look means. You're about to hatch an elaborate plan that involves a lot of hugging, singing, dancing and *glitter!*" He said the last word through tightly clenched teeth.

Poppy grinned from ear to ear. "You know it!"

Branch held up his hands, this time in a calming gesture. "Poppy, please," he said quietly. "I'm going home now. Promise me you'll sleep on it before you rush into something, like you always do."

"Okay," Poppy promised. "I won't do anything."

＊

But that night, Poppy lay in her bed with her eyes wide open and shining in the dark. She couldn't possibly sleep. She was way too excited about her idea! She tossed and turned.

A big part of her wanted to jump up and put her new plan into action right away. But she'd promised Branch she wouldn't do that.

Still, she couldn't just keep tossing and turning and turning and tossing. And *thinking*.

Poppy got out of bed and tapped a Glowfly. "Thank you," she said to the critter as warm, soft light filled the room. "Sorry, I know it's late."

"No problem," the bug fluted in a high-pitched voice. "I couldn't sleep anyway."

"Me either!" Poppy said, shaking her head.

She tried several methods to make herself sleepy. She took a hot bath. She drank a cup of warm milk. She told herself a story. She sang herself a lullaby.

Nothing worked. She still felt wide awake.

Finally, Poppy gave up on sleeping. She walked over to the big wooden trunk where she kept all her scrapbooking materials and opened it.

❄

The next morning, Branch woke up early and made himself a nice cup of bloomingflower tea. He'd slept so soundly, even his dreams were about sleeping. Sipping his tea and quietly humming to himself, he took the lift down to the basement of his bunker. He wore a robe and sported a serious case of bedhead. He yawned so widely, it seemed as though his head would split in half.

Suddenly, someone said, "GOOD MORNING, BRANCH!"

"YAAAAH!" Branch screamed. Startled by the voice, he spilled his tea all over himself.

It was Poppy. And she looked very excited. More so than usual. Branch frowned. That could only mean trouble ... for him.

"Poppy," he said sternly. "You didn't sleep on it. You probably didn't sleep at all."

"Not a wink," Poppy agreed, grinning.

"And you've probably got a crazy plan," Branch growled.

"Yes, I do," Poppy chirped. "Except it's not crazy. I decided the Bergens need a new holiday!"

"Okay, let's send a card telling them that," Branch said, wiping his face with his robe. "Problem solved."

"Wait, that's not my *whole* idea!" Poppy continued. "No one knows holidays better than us Trolls! So we'll just give the Bergens one of

our holidays! Brilliant, huh?"

Branch looked confused. "And why are we doing this?"

Poppy picked up Branch's cup and poured him a fresh cup of tea. "Bridget is my *best friend*," she said. "The Bergens deserve to have a day of dancing and singing, costumes and presents ... and glitter!" Forgetting she'd poured the tea for Branch, she took a swig of it herself as she relished the idea of glitter. "So much glitter."

"Are you sure this is a good idea?" Branch asked.

"Absolutely!" Poppy said. "This is what I do. I take care of my friends."

Branch thought about it for a minute. Then he said, "You know what? Old Branch would probably not be into this plan at all, but New Branch, with his cool new smile—"

He tried smiling again. It came out crooked.

"Still weird," Poppy said, offering him the cup of tea.

"Huh," Branch said. "I'll keep working on it." He took the cup of tea from her and blew on it to cool it down. "So what's your plan?"

Poppy pulled out a scrapbook. "I've assembled a well-thought-out plan in here." She held the book up for Branch to see, turning the pages as she explained.

"It's simple," she went on. "First, break into Branch's bunker and get him on board."

A little felt figure of Branch on the first page gave her a big thumbs-up. "I'm on board!" the tiny Branch said.

Branch couldn't believe Poppy had known ahead of time that he would agree to her idea. But he didn't say anything. He just shook his head.

"Next," Poppy said, turning the page, "we set

off for Bergen Town. Once we get there, we'll—"

"How will we get there, exactly?" Branch interrupted. "We're too heavy for the Zip Beetles to carry us and I don't think you want to go through what you did the first time you went to Bergen Town … falling off a flower, riding on a snake, being swallowed by a bird and a fish and a plant—"

"How do you know about all that?" Poppy asked. "You weren't even there for those parts!"

Branch held up another scrapbook. "You scrapbooked the whole thing, remember?"

"Oh, yeah!" Poppy said, reaching for it. "I *wondered* where that went!" She squinted at Branch, puzzled. "Were you keeping this as a souvenir of our adventure together?"

Branch looked like he'd been caught. "Uh, no! Of course not! I just wanted to make sure it got back to Troll Village safely, that's all. Anyway, you were telling me how you plan to get to Bergen Town this time. More comfortably, I hope."

"Oh, most def," Poppy said, flipping through the pages of her new plan. She found the page she was looking for and held it up for Branch to admire. "This time we'll go by Caterbus!"

The page showed a bunch of felt Trolls lining up to board a felt bus that looked a lot like a giant caterpillar. Poppy turned to the next page, which showed King Gristle and Bridget on their thrones.

"We'll see Gristle and Bridget and do some hugging!" she said. She flipped the next page back and forth, making it look like Poppy and Bridget were hugging over and over.

"I get it," Branch said. "You'll hug. And then?"

"We'll pitch them our holiday ideas," Poppy said. "Their minds will be blown."

One page showed rainbows shooting out of King

Gristle's and Bridget's heads.

"And that's how we're going to give Bridget and the rest of the Bergens a new holiday!" The last page of Poppy's elaborate scrapbook shot out a puff of glitter and happy little voices sang, *"Holiday!"*

Behind Branch, a bunch of Poppy's friends, including Biggie, Smidge, Guy Diamond, Fuzzbert, Satin, Chenille and Cooper had stepped out of the shadows to join in, singing along with Poppy's scrapbook.

"AAAHHHH!" Branch screamed, spilling tea all over himself again. His robe was soaked. He looked down at it, then up at all the Trolls who had somehow sneaked into his bunker.

"I figure we need a team of holiday experts to make our presentation," Poppy explained, grinning.

"Looks like we're all headed to Bergen Town." Branch sighed. "I'll go and put on some trousers."

CHAPTER
4

In a forest clearing at the edge of Troll Village, Poppy, Branch and their friends waited for the Caterbus to arrive. They were eager to share their holiday ideas with the Bergens.

"Is the Caterbus absolutely safe?" Biggie asked nervously. "I mean, I'm not worried, but sometimes Mr Dinkles gets all worked up when he travels."

"Zzzzz…" Mr Dinkles snored, lying on Biggie's shoulder.

"Oh, I'm sure it's perfectly safe," Poppy reassured him, patting her big friend's back. "In fact, they say

it's the safest way to travel!"

"Who says that?" Branch asked sceptically. "The Caterbus driver?"

"Yes," Poppy admitted. "But who would know better? He rides Caterbuses all the time!"

Before Branch could argue with Poppy's logic, the Caterbus came roaring around a corner and lurched to a stop just centimetres from where they were standing. *SCREEEEEEECH!*

"AAAAAHHHH!" Branch screamed for the third time that morning.

The Caterbus looked a lot like a huge caterpillar, with lots of sections and two antennae in front. The door opened wide, and a voice announced, "BUUUUSSS!"

Poppy didn't hesitate. She jumped right onto the Caterbus and encouraged the other Trolls to follow her. "Come on, everybody! All aboard!"

They piled onto the bus. Some liked to sit up front, while others preferred the seats in the back. There was plenty of room for everybody. The inside was decorated in bright colours – red, orange and yellow. Soft to sit on, the seats were sparkly purple with rainbow armrests.

Poppy and Branch found a two-Troll seat near the front. They sat and buckled their seat belts.

A voice, mimicking a deep echo, announced, "Welcome ... welcome ... welcome ... to ... to ... to ... the Caterbus Express ... ess ... ess..."

"Wait a minute," Branch said. "Making his own echo? Where have I heard that voice before?" Then he remembered! "Oh, no ... not him." He looked towards the driver's seat, hoping he was wrong about the voice, but then he saw—

Cloud Guy! White and puffy, he wore his usual striped sports socks, but he'd added a snappy blue-

and-gold driver's cap with a black brim.

Branch moaned. He was not fond of Cloud Guy. When Branch and Poppy had needed to find the tunnel that led to Bergen Town, Cloud Guy had refused to help unless Branch gave him a high five. And a fist bump. And a hug. It had gone on until Branch had "persuaded" Cloud Guy to show them the way by chasing him with a sharp stick.

And now Cloud Guy was going to drive them to Bergen Town on the Caterbus. He sat behind the steering wheel, grinning back at Branch.

"Hey, guys," he said in his friendly voice. "Captain No-Slappy." He nodded at Branch, referring to the missed high five. "Queen Poppy."

Poppy was delighted to see Cloud Guy. She thought he was funny – and they shared a certain joy in playfully teasing Branch.

"All right, Cloud Guy," she said. "Punch it!"

"You got it," Cloud Guy drawled. "But first, a quick announcement." He spoke into the speaking tube of the Caterbus's speaker system. "Please put away all electronics, safely stow your carry-ons and hold on to your Dinkles."

Fuzzbert took off his headphones and put them away. Cooper stowed tiny Smidge in an overhead compartment (she enjoyed the snug privacy). And Biggie gave Mr Dinkles a loving squeeze.

"Mew," Mr Dinkles said.

"Thank you for choosing the Caterbus," Cloud Guy concluded. "The safest way to travel!" He hung up the speaking tube and mumbled, "Unless we go into a wormhole."

Branch pricked up his big ears. "I'm sorry ... did you just say *wormhole*?"

Cloud Guy ignored him. "Now sit back, relax and feel the love. Next stop, Bergen Town ... town

... town!" He jammed his foot down on the pedal and the Caterbus leapt forward! *VROOOOOM!*

The long Caterbus zoomed through the woods, whipping around trees, rocks and bushes. *Most* of the rocks and bushes, anyway. It bumped right over the rest, sending the Trolls flying out of their seats. It twisted and turned, not following any road or path that Branch could see.

"CAREFUL! WATCH WHERE YOU'RE GOING!" Branch shouted. "SLOW DOWN!"

But instead of slowing down, Cloud Guy reached out and pushed a button. Loud, pulsing music blasted through the Caterbus. Cloud Guy knew the Trolls couldn't resist a good tune with a catchy beat. *And* it would drown out Branch's complaints.

He was right. All the Trolls (except Branch) jumped to their feet and danced in the aisle, swerving with the rocking motion of the Caterbus. *"YEAH!"*

they sang along as they danced. *"NO NEED TO MAKE A GREAT BIG FUSS ... WHEN YOU'RE RIDIN' ON THE CATERBUS! DANCE, DANCE, DANCE, YEAH – ALL OF US!"*

Only Branch stayed safely buckled into his seat. He watched his friends gyrate, twist, kick and pump their fists to the music. Finally, he couldn't resist – Branch jumped up and joined the dance. They all moved and grooved in a line until Branch noticed that someone else had joined in too.

Cloud Guy!

"WHO'S DRIVING THE BUS?" Branch cried out!

Everyone stopped dancing and looked at Cloud Guy. He grinned and shrugged ... just as the Caterbus plunged off the edge of a cliff!

"YAAAAAHHHHHHH!" they screamed.

CHAPTER
5

The Caterbus plummeted through the air until a gigantic creature opened its cavernous mouth and swallowed the Caterbus up. *GULP!*

"WORMHOLE!" Cloud Guy yelled.

"What?" Branch asked.

Cloud Guy turned to him and repeated calmly, "Wormhole. We've just been swallowed by one. I suggest you remain seated with your seat belt fastened—"

But before he could finish his sentence, Cloud Guy was sent flying as the Caterbus twisted and turned through the dark tunnels inside the huge, mysterious wormhole. Weird images flashed outside the windows – swirling patterns and flashing lights.

The Trolls were flung about the Caterbus, bouncing off the seats and the ceiling.

"AAAAAHHHH!" Biggie screamed.

"WAAAHH!" Cooper shouted.

"Eeeee!" Mr Dinkles squeaked.

"WOOOOOAAAA!" Smidge bellowed in her deep voice.

Cloud Guy laughed like a maniac. "MWAH-HA-HA-HA-HA-HA!"

Rainbow-coloured lights blinked outside. After a blinding flash of white light, everything went still. Eerily still...

The Caterbus seemed to be floating through the darkness of empty space. Stars twinkled in the distance. A meteor blazed above and then disappeared.

A figure in a spacesuit floated by. It turned and just for a moment, the figure in the suit seemed to be a Troll. But how was that possible? Where were they? And what was happening?

Inside the dark Caterbus, Cooper slowly waved his foot in front of his face. It left behind a rainbow trail that hung in the air.

"You guys?" he said. "I don't feel so good..."

Peering at his foot from beneath the brim of his green hat, Cooper blinked. His foot looked strange. Instead of being soft and fuzzy, it looked hard, smooth and shiny. It seemed to be made out of ... squishy rubber!

"What's wrong, Cooper?" Biggie asked.

Cooper turned to his left and saw that Biggie had turned into a big rubber doll! He looked to his right and saw that the same thing had happened to Guy Diamond!

"I'm feeling weird..." Guy said, his voice reverberating.

"Me too!" Biggie added.

"Wem!" Mr Dinkles said.

"'Wem?' What does that mean?" Guy Diamond asked.

"I think it's 'mew' backwards," Biggie explained. "I guess Mr Dinkles is feeling weird, too. Poor little guy. Don't worry, Mr Dinkles. Everything'll be all right! I'm here!"

FLASH! There was another blinding burst of white light. Blinking, the Trolls looked at each other. They gasped! ALL of them had turned into dolls! Even Mr Dinkles!

"AAAHHHHH!" they screamed.

"MWAH-HA-HA-HA-HA!" laughed Cloud Guy as his head started to spin around and around.

FLASH! There was another burst of light, and

then the Caterbus went into a nosedive! It rocketed past stars, planets, asteroids and moons as it fell through space.

"AAAAAHHH!" the Trolls screamed again.

Biggie looked at Cooper. "At least we're back to normal!" he observed.

"Yeah," Cooper agreed. "We don't look like dolls any more. However, on the downside, we're falling through space!"

"But we never went into space, did we?" asked Biggie. "How is this *possible*?"

"It's because we're inside the WORMHOLE!" Cloud Guy explained, still laughing wildly. "In the WORMHOLE, *anything's* possible!"

"Even lunch?" Smidge asked hopefully. "I'm starving!"

Before Cloud Guy could answer, the view through the windows of the Caterbus shifted from black space to violet space. There was nothing but purple as far as the eye could see!

Then the colour outside shifted again, this time to indigo and then to blue.

"Beautiful!" Poppy said, trying to make the best of a baffling situation. "It's like we're flying through a giant rainbow! And rainbows are ALWAYS good! Right?"

"Not when you're *falling* through one!" Branch grumbled.

The space outside the Caterbus turned to green, then yellow, then orange and then red.

"Isn't red the last colour in the rainbow?" Cooper asked. "Maybe we're getting close to the end of the wormhole."

"Then what happens?" Biggie asked, frightened.

But the solid-red space outside the Caterbus windows wasn't the last zone they passed through.

Next came stripes, then chequers and then polka dots—

"I love all these patterns!" Satin exclaimed.

"It looks like material for dresses!" Chenille agreed.

"Or trouser suits!" Satin added.

"I don't know," Biggie moaned, clutching his stomach. "All these crazy patterns are making me kind of queasy."

WHOOSH! The Caterbus broke through the patterns into a beautiful blue sky.

"Ladies and gentlemen, we are out of the wormhole!" Cloud Guy announced.

The Trolls cheered! Except Branch, who shouted, "But we're still FALLING!"

"That's true," Cooper said. "Good point. Let's panic! YAAAAAAHHHH!"

The Caterbus plummeted through the blue

sky, plunging past clouds and birds. Through the windscreen, the Trolls could see the solid ground coming up fast!

"This is it!" Biggie wailed. "GOODBYE, MR DINKLES! GOODBYE, EVERYONE!"

They all braced themselves, holding on to their seats. But just before they crashed, the front of the Caterbus pulled up and it flew neatly over the ground, skimming along and then touching down for a perfect soft landing.

"We're on the ground!" Cloud Guy announced. "I *told* you the Caterbus was the safest way to travel!"

Everyone cheered! They were safe.

Cloud Guy reached up and pulled down his speaking tube. "Trolls and Troll pets, this is your driver speaking. Let me be the first to welcome you to the ground. We here at Caterbus Express know you have a choice in travel lines, so we appreciate your business. Please remember to remove all personal items—"

"But where exactly ARE we?" Branch interrupted.

It was a very good question.

CHAPTER
6

The Trolls looked out at a strange landscape that was different from any they'd ever seen before. The trees and stones were oddly shaped and the colours seemed off.

"Mighty pretty country," Cloud Guy drawled, trying to put a positive spin on the situation.

"Okay, but again, my point: WHERE ARE WE?" Branch asked.

Cloud Guy shrugged. "Dunno. Wormholes move around a lot. Could be anywhere. Not Bergen Town, that's for sure."

"I can see that!" Branch said.

"Okay, everybody!" Poppy said brightly. "Let's get off this Caterbus and find out where we are! C'mon!"

"Wait a minute," Branch said. "Are you sure it's safe out there? Should we all just jump off the bus and into the unknown?"

Poppy put her hands on her hips. "Well, what's the alternative, Branch? Live on this Caterbus for ever?"

"That could work," Branch said.

"Cloud Guy," Poppy said. "Please open the door. Slowly, if possible."

Cloud Guy pushed a lever and the big front door swung open. Poppy led the way, confidently striding off the Caterbus. The others followed cautiously, looking around, listening carefully.

When they got outside, they stood in a clump and stared at the world around them. In the near distance, they could see three different landscapes. In one direction was a snowy, mountainous land. In another they saw a deep, dark forest. And in the third direction were rolling green meadows.

Branch pointed towards the meadows. "Well, that way *looks* friendly and inviting, but you just know it's going to turn out to be horrible and terrible once you get there."

Cloud Guy smiled and nodded. "Right. Could easily be the way to CERTAIN DEATH ... death ... death ... death."

"Or at least imprisonment," Branch countered.

"Sure," Cloud Guy agreed. "Could be imprisonment. Definitely."

"*Followed* by death," Branch said.

"Or MAYBE," Poppy argued, "it could turn out to be just as nice and safe as it looks!"

"Maybe," Cloud Guy said sceptically.

"Doubt it," Branch added.

"So, which way will get us to Bergen Town?" Biggie asked.

They all looked at Cloud Guy. He just stood there smiling. Then he realized they expected him to answer.

"Oh!" he exclaimed. "You're asking *me*?"

"Yes!" Biggie said. "You're the driver!"

"That's true," Cloud Guy said, taking a moment to consider exactly what his passenger responsibilities were. "Well, let me see…" He looked in each direction. He licked his finger and stuck it in the air to test the wind. He took a deep sniff. He got down on his hands and knees and listened to the ground for a long time. Then he stood up and smiled.

"No idea. We're totally lost."

The Trolls started to panic, frightened that they'd

never get to Bergen Town or back home. Tears rolled down Biggie's cheeks.

Poppy and Branch took charge.

"Don't worry," Poppy reassured her friends. "We're not going to stay lost. We're going to find our way out of here and get to Bergen Town!"

"Poppy's right," Branch said. "There's no need to panic."

"Actually, I'm pretty sure there is!" Biggie sobbed. *"We're hopelessly lost!"*

Poppy reached up to pat Biggie on the back. "Lost, but not hopelessly. We're *full* of hope!"

"We are?" Biggie asked uncertainly.

"Sure!" Poppy insisted. "We just have to figure out which way leads to Bergen Town. We'll split into three scouting teams."

"Good idea," Branch said.

"Cloud Guy, you're with me and Branch," Poppy

said. "We'll check out the snow zone."

"Cool," Cloud Guy said. *"Literally."*

Branch rolled his eyes. "Wait a minute..." he objected, not fond of the idea of being on a search team with Cloud Guy.

But Poppy had already turned to the next team. "Biggie, Cooper and Smidge, you investigate that forest."

"You got it, Poppy!" Smidge said with deep-voiced gusto. With her tremendous strength, there wasn't much that scared the little Troll. Biggie and Cooper, on the other hand, exchanged a nervous look.

"Satin, Chenille and Fuzzbert," Poppy continued, "you go take a look at those rolling green meadows."

Satin raised her hand. "But didn't Branch say that way could turn out to be..."

"... horrible and terrible?" her twin said, finishing the question with her hand raised too.

"He said it *could* turn out to be horrible and terrible," Poppy said. "But it could just as easily turn out to be wonderful and delightful! *Right?*"

The fashionable twins didn't look too sure. But they loved their queen and her confidence gave them confidence. They were willing to be brave if she needed them to be. They nodded.

"Okay, teams," Branch said. "We'll meet back here at the Caterbus to report our findings."

"What about me?" Guy Diamond asked.

Biggie handed Mr Dinkles to the glittery Troll. "You stay here and take care of Mr Dinkles. I don't want to carry him into danger!"

"Mew?" Mr Dinkles asked, his eyes growing wide with uncertainty.

Trudging through deep snow, Poppy, Branch and

Cloud Guy slowly made their way towards the mountains.

"This snow is beautiful!" Poppy enthused. "Look at it sparkle in the sunshine!"

"It's also cold!" Branch complained. "What are we looking for exactly? A road?"

"A sign saying 'This Way to Bergen Town' would be nice," Cloud Guy suggested.

"I'm thinking we'll run into a friendly stranger who'll point the way," Poppy chirped. "And give us hot chocolate!"

They met no one as they tromped on through the snow on the ground. And then it started snowing…

But it wasn't normal snow.

WHAM! WHOMP! THWUMP! Gigantic snowflakes fell from the sky and stuck into the ground on their sharp points. Each flake stood twice as high as a Troll!

"Watch out!" Branch called as they dodged the huge flakes. "Don't let one of them bonk you on the head! It could be deadly!" *WHAM!*

The snowfall stopped as quickly as it had begun, but it left behind a barrier of upright snowflakes. Picking their way around them, the Trolls felt like they were trying to solve a maze.

"You know, this really isn't fun at all," Cloud Guy observed as he trailed behind the two Trolls.

They got clear of the big snowflakes, but the situation got worse. Another storm began, but this time giant icicles fell from the sky! *SHWUNK! SHWUNK! SHWUNK!* They fell straight into the snow like spears! The Trolls and Cloud Guy had to run in zigzags to dodge the plummeting icicles.

"The weather around here is really terrible," Cloud Guy said.

"Yeah – can't you do anything about it?" Branch

asked as he jumped out of the path of another colossal icicle. *SHWUNK!*

"Why me?" Cloud Guy asked.

"BECAUSE YOU'RE A CLOUD!" Branch shouted.

"Cloud *Guy*," he corrected. "There's a difference."

Luckily, they managed to escape the icicles, and the storm didn't last long. When they got past the last icicle stuck in the snow, they realized they were close to the base of a frozen mountain. Cloud Guy shaded his eyes with his hand and peered ahead.

"I see something coming," he said.

"A friendly stranger with mugs of steaming cocoa and frothy cream?" Poppy asked hopefully. "And a light dusting of chocolate powder?"

"Nope," Cloud Guy said, "a huge snowball. And it's rolling this way."

CHAPTER
7

He was right. An enormous snowball was rolling straight at them. And two more were coming right behind it!

"RUN!" Branch yelled, somewhat unnecessarily, since Poppy and Cloud Guy were already sprinting to get out of the way.

FWOOM! FWOOM! FWOOM! The three snowballs rushed by them, picking up more snow as they went, growing and growing, until they crashed into the field of icicles the Trolls had left behind. *SMASH!*

"Where did those giant snowballs come from?" Poppy asked, shocked.

"I'm guessing those guys," Cloud Guy said, pointing up the mountain.

Poppy and Branch looked up and saw large, fierce-looking creatures covered in long white hair. Thin legs and antennae extended from their bodies. Sliding down the side of the mountain on sheets of bark, the hairy beasts headed straight towards the Trolls and Cloud Guy, growling and snarling.

"Who are *they*?" Branch asked.

"Freezybeasts," Cloud Guy answered. "And from what I've heard, they're *not* friendly."

While Poppy, Branch and Cloud Guy were struggling through the snowy foothills of the frozen mountains, Biggie, Cooper and Smidge were hiking into the dark woods. They soon found themselves in a thick forest of Troll-sized fir trees.

"It *smells* nice in here," Biggie said, drawing in the sweet air through his nose. "Piney!"

"It *smells* nice," Smidge agreed, "but it's tricky to walk through!"

She was right. Growing out of the ground were vines and shoots that wrapped around the trees like pieces of tinsel. Other plants formed themselves into shiny ribbons and bows. The Trolls had to make their way through thick knots and tangles.

At first, Biggie led the way. He was the biggest, so he tried to clear a path for the other two Trolls to follow. But the decorative undergrowth was too dense for him to plough through and soon he was stuck!

"Here, let *me* try!" Cooper said. "I've got twice as many legs to run on!"

"I don't quite see how that's going to help," Biggie said.

"Just watch!" Cooper cried as he backed up, got a running start and ploughed right into the undergrowth, churning his four legs as fast as he could.

But in no time, he was stuck, too, hopelessly tangled up in the vines and shoots.

"*Um*, a little help?" he said weakly.

Using the great strength of her hair, Smidge pulled Cooper out of the jumbled mass of shining greenery. With maximum effort, they managed to pull Biggie free too.

"Thanks!" Biggie gasped. "Smidge, maybe you could somehow clear a path with your hair."

"How?" Smidge asked.

"Whip it around like you're whacking weeds!" Cooper suggested. "That's *sure* to work!"

Moving her little head in a circle, Smidge whipped her hair around faster and faster until it was a blue blur.

"Okay, great!" Cooper called to her. "Now use it to clear a path!"

Smidge moved towards the thick undergrowth, put her head down – and almost instantly got her long hair tangled up in the plants!

"Uh-oh." Biggie sighed. "Who's good at untying knots?"

"Pirates?" Cooper guessed.

At the same time that the first party was trudging through snow and the second party was getting tangled up in vines, the third party was happily skipping through the beautiful meadows.

"This is…" Satin began.

"… so fun!" Chenille finished. The twins joined hands, laughing.

Fuzzbert giggled, his laughter muffled by the long green hair that covered his whole body.

"It's very nice, but how are we supposed to find the way to Bergen Town?" Satin asked as they strolled through the cool, soft grass. A light, warm breeze blew. The air smelled like flowers.

"Look!" said Chenille, pointing ahead. "Maybe they know the way!"

Fuzzbert and Satin looked to see what she meant. They saw a crowd of critters and they were all singing! It was a choir of musical critters – Tunebugs, Chimers, Critterchords, Chorusflies, Humworms, Chanters – just about every kind of musical critter there was. Their song filled the air with buggy melodies and harmonies.

The Trolls quickly made their way over to the critter choir.

"Excuse us," Satin said.

All the critters stopped singing. They turned and stared at the Trolls with bulging eyes.

"Do you happen to know the way to Bergen Town?" Chenille asked. "We're kind of lost."

"As in..." Satin began.

"... totally," Chenille finished.

The critters looked at each other, wiggling their antennae and petals. The Trolls got the feeling the critters might be saying something in their own secret language. Then one of the Critterchords stepped forward.

"Do you ... sing?" it asked.

Satin grinned. "Well, sure! Trolls *love* to sing!"

The musical critters smiled and nodded.

The Critterchord said, "We will be glad to tell you the way. But first – sing with us!"

The Trolls looked at each other and shrugged. If it meant getting directions to Bergen Town, they guessed they had time to sing a song or two...

But after singing many, many, *many* songs with

the critter choir, the Trolls had had enough. Their voices were getting tired. And they needed to find their way to Bergen Town.

"Well, that was fun," Chenille croaked. "But we've really got to get going. If you could point us towards Bergen Town—"

"You all sing very well," a Tunebug interrupted.

"We like to sing with you," buzzed a Chorusfly.

Fuzzbert made some grunting sounds that the Trolls understood to mean, "Thank you very much."

"But now…" said Satin hoarsely.

"… it's time for us to go," Chenille said in a rasp.

The musical critters looked at each other and quickly formed a ring around the Trolls.

"No," the Critterchord insisted. "You are in our choir now. You will stay and sing with us. *For ever!*"

CHAPTER 8

Poppy, Branch and Cloud Guy watched the hairy Freezybeasts slide down the mountain straight towards them, their bark sledges kicking up clouds of snow.

"We've got to get to Bergen Town to help Bridget," Poppy said. "Maybe they know the way!"

"Or *maybe* they know the way to cook Trolls!" Branch replied, exasperated.

"And Cloud Guys," added Cloud Guy.

"Yes, and Cloud Guys," Branch said. "So I'm thinking we RUN!"

They turned and ran, not back the way they'd come, but towards the deep forest where Biggie, Cooper and Smidge had gone. They picked through the rocks and boulders that had rolled down the mountain, trying to stay low so the Freezybeasts couldn't see them.

But when they looked back, they saw the Freezybeasts jump off their sledges and chase them on their long, spindly legs, still hooting and barking. The ones in front sniffed the air as though they were following the Trolls' scent.

"We've got to lose these hairy dudes!" Cloud Guy gasped, holding his side as he ran. "But how?"

"We can lose them in the forest," Poppy said, breathing hard.

"I don't think we'll make it," Branch said. "The woods are too far. They'll catch up with us before we get there."

Poppy pointed ahead. "Look! Over there!" She was indicating a patch of briars and brambles.

"That doesn't look very comfy," Cloud Guy said.

"Yeah, but I'm betting those hairy Freezybeasts won't like it, either," Poppy said. "Come on! And keep your hair up high, Branch!"

"Right!" he answered as they ran towards the prickly patch.

"Guys! Are we sure about this?" Cloud Guy called.

"Yes!" Poppy and Branch answered together.

Keeping their hair high so it wouldn't get caught in the brambles, Poppy and Branch scrambled into the thorny patch, trying to avoid getting scratched. Cloud Guy went in a little more slowly and reluctantly, but he went.

The Freezybeasts came roaring up, but when they saw the thicket of briar, they slid to a stop.

They were familiar with the bramble patch and had no desire to go in. Their long white hair would catch on the thorns and get plucked out, painfully. Without a word, they turned around and went back to their mountain caves to do whatever it was that Freezybeasts did.

Poppy, Branch and Cloud Guy were happy to see the Freezybeasts go. But they were even happier when they exited the briar thicket and saw a road running between the thicket and the dark forest.

"Could this be the road to Bergen Town?" Poppy asked.

Cloud Guy knelt and studied the road. Then he stood up and grinned. "You know what? I think it is. Totes!"

"That's great!" Poppy exclaimed.

"Now we just have to tell the others, get back to the Caterbus and drive to Bergen Town!" Branch said.

They crossed the road and headed into the dark forest, calling for their friends.

"Biggie!" Poppy called, cupping her hands around her mouth.

"Smidge!" Branch shouted.

"Dudes! And lady-Troll dudes!" Cloud Guy called.

As they walked along, the going got tougher with more and more undergrowth.

"You know," Poppy said, "these plants may be hard to walk through, but they sure are pretty. They look like ribbons and bows and garlands."

"Yeah," Cloud Guy said, "ribbons and bows and garlands that get all tangled up around your ankles."

"*Shhh!*" Branch hissed, holding up a hand. "I think I hear something!"

They stood there for a moment, listening. Then

they clearly heard three of their friends calling, "HELP!"

They hurried through the shadowy woods as best they could until they found Biggie, Cooper and Smidge. Their friends were thoroughly tangled up in some dark green vines.

"Poppy! Branch!" Biggie said, tears running down his cheeks. "Thank goodness you're here!"

"And what about me?" Cloud Guy asked, a little hurt.

"I don't really know you that well," Biggie explained bashfully.

Branch, Poppy and Cloud Guy went straight to work untangling the Trolls, careful not to get tangled up themselves. It wasn't easy. It almost seemed as though the vines *wanted* to tie themselves into bows and knots.

"We sure could use some pirates to help untie

these knots," Cloud Guy muttered.

"That's what *I* said!" Cooper said, glad that someone knew what he was talking about.

Once the three were freed from their leafy bindings, all six of them headed out to find the team that had gone into the meadows.

"Walk closely together," Poppy warned. "That way we'll trample a path together."

They managed to make it out of the forest. Behind them, the vines they'd stepped on sprang right back up, ready to form themselves into new bows and garlands.

As the friends hurried into the rolling green meadows, they heard singing in the distance.

"Is that ... a choir?" Biggie asked.

"Sounds like it," Poppy said. "And I think I can make out Satin's and Chenille's voices! But they sound hoarse."

"Oh, sure," Branch complained. "While we're getting snowed on and chased by Freezybeasts and tangled up in vines, they're having choir practice!"

The friends hurried across the soft green grass. As they came over a low hill, they saw a circle of critters singing. In the centre of the circle were Satin, Chenille and Fuzzbert!

"Guys!" Poppy called. "Over here! We found a road!"

The musical critters turned around and stared at the newcomers.

"Oooh," the Critterchord said. "More Trolls!"

"Poppy!" Satin shouted. "Save us!"

The five Trolls and Cloud Guy reached the circle of critters.

"Do you sing?" the Critterchord asked.

Before the captured Trolls could warn her, Poppy cheerfully blurted, "Of course we do! All Trolls sing!"

A Tunebug pointed at Cloud Guy. "Are you a Troll?"

Cloud Guy looked taken aback. "No! I'm Cloud Guy. You can call me Cloud Guy."

"Do you sing?" the Tunebug asked.

Cloud Guy looked a little smug. "Do *I* sing? You betcha! I'm just about the *best* singer you've ever heard! Here, I'll prove it!" He started to sing a song about clouds. *"Every time I see a cloud, I have got to sing out loud! They make me oh so very proud to be a part of the cloudy crowd…"*

Cloud Guy had an amazing voice. But he was loud. Really loud.

In fact, he was so loud, several critters' faces scrunched up. Others covered their ears with their feet. Some of them fell to the ground.

"Stop!" they cried. "STOP!"

But Cloud Guy kept singing. Branch saw a

chance for their friends to escape from the critters' choir.

"Come on!" he whispered to the four Trolls inside the circle. "Let's get out of here!" He turned to Cloud Guy. "Keep singing!"

And he did. His song about clouds seemed to have about as many verses as there are clouds in the sky. On a very cloudy day.

As the critters writhed on the ground, tortured by Cloud Guy's thundering vocals, the Trolls slipped away. Poppy took Cloud Guy by the hand.

"We're leaving!" she said.

"But I haven't finished my song!" he protested.

"You can keep singing," Poppy said. "Just come with us. In fact, keep singing until we're back on the Caterbus. It'll keep us safe."

"You mean entertained?" Cloud Guy asked.

"Yeah," Poppy said hesitantly. "Entertained."

As Cloud Guy continued to sing, he and the Trolls ran back to the Caterbus. They climbed on, greeting Guy Diamond and Mr Dinkles, and persuaded Cloud Guy to stop singing and start driving. He headed for the road they'd spotted between the briar patch and the deep forest.

"I just hope it's the right road," Branch said.

CHAPTER 9

The Caterbus barrelled along, kicking up dust and gravel. The Trolls were eager to quickly put as much distance as possible between themselves and the three treacherous landscapes they'd just escaped. They'd had enough of Freezybeasts, tangling vines and singing critters.

"This is starting to look familiar," Cloud Guy said as he steered the bus along the dusty road. He spotted something up ahead. "There! THE TUNNELS!"

Through the windscreen, the Trolls sitting in

front could see the underground tunnels that led to the old Troll Tree in Bergen Town. They cheered as Cloud Guy drove the Caterbus into one of them. Biggie hugged Mr Dinkles.

"Next stop, Bergen Town!" Cloud Guy said. "Unless I've got the wrong tunnel. In which case, CERTAIN DEATH … death … death …"

"I really wish he'd stop doing that echo thing," Branch whispered to Poppy.

"Me too," she whispered back.

But Cloud Guy had picked the right tunnel, and soon the Caterbus shot out of the middle of the Troll Tree, flying through the air towards the castle in Bergen Town!

One Bergen looked up and saw it. "What's that?" he asked.

Another Bergen looked up. "Caterbus. From Troll Village. Looks like an express," he said calmly.

"Wanna play that game where we throw the die and move around the square?"

"No."

"Neither do I."

WHOMP! The Caterbus landed at the base of the stairs leading up to the castle's front door. Cloud Guy opened the Caterbus door and the Trolls spilled out.

"Thanks, Cloud Guy!" Poppy said.

"Yeah, thanks a lot for letting go of the steering wheel so we plunged off a cliff and fell into a wormhole," Branch said sarcastically.

"You're welcome!" Cloud Guy said cheerfully, mistaking it for a compliment. "Anytime!" As he closed the door, Cloud Guy started singing again. *"Every time I see a cloud…"*

The Trolls covered their ears. The Caterbus roared off. *VRRRROOOOM!*

With Poppy leading the way, the Trolls quickly went into the castle and through the halls to the throne room. They were so much smaller than the Bergen guards that Todd and Chad didn't even notice them pass by.

The Trolls huddled outside the throne room's big doors, where Poppy reminded her friends of their roles for the presentation.

"Okay. Guy Diamond, you're on glitter."

"Glitter at the ready!" he said, saluting. "Let it shine!"

"Cooper," Poppy said, "pyrotechnics."

"Huh?" Cooper said. "I thought I was doing the fireworks."

"Pyrotechnics *are* fireworks," Branch explained.

"Oh," Cooper said. "In that case, ready!" He gave a confident nod and a welding mask fell down over his face. He raised a blowtorch, which was

already lit and flaming.

"Satin, Chenille," Poppy continued, "festive outfits."

"On it!" the twins said at the same time. They'd already dressed Branch in a pair of baggy trousers with suspenders. He didn't look thrilled.

"Uh, Poppy, about these costumes…" he began.

"Branch, we've been over this," Poppy said firmly. "It's not a holiday without costumes! So pull up your big-boy trousers and let's get in there!"

"Yes, but—"

"Sorry, Branch, it's show time! Ready, everybody?" Poppy held up her fingers as she counted down. "In three … two …. one … LET'S GO!"

BOOM! The Trolls burst into the throne room. A painting fell to the floor. *CRASH!*

"STOP EVERYTHING!" Poppy shouted.

Bridget looked up from her magazine, and Gristle stopped playing his keyboard. Under their thrones, Barnabus, their pet crocodile, stopped gnawing on a discarded slice of pizza. All three stared at Poppy, wondering what the emergency was.

"Huh?" King Gristle asked. "What's going on?"

"Sorry," Poppy said sheepishly. "I got a little carried away with the whole 'Stop everything!' thing."

"Poppy!" Bridget squealed, delighted to see her friend.

"Bridget!" Poppy exclaimed.

The two friends greeted each other with hugs and elaborate handshakes and high fives, calling each other by the nicknames they'd made up together.

"Pop Star!"

"B-Bop!"

"Lollipop!"

"Roller Girl!"

"Glitter Bomb!"

"Morning Jogger!"

"Helicopter!"

"Prim and Proper!"

Branch and King Gristle greeted each other too, but kept their greetings much more low-key. Nodding to each other, Gristle said, "'Sup," and Branch replied, "'Sup."

Poppy noticed that Bridget had new rainbow-coloured extensions attached to her pigtails.

"Your hair looks amazing!" she told her friend.

"Why, thank you!" Bridget said. Then she leaned over and whispered, *"It's a weave."*

"I won't say a word," Poppy whispered back.

"It's so good to see you, Poppy!" Bridget said at a normal volume. "Um, what are you doing here?"

Poppy took that as her cue to begin the

presentation. "Funny you should ask," she said. "Smidge, HIT THE LIGHTS!"

The room went dark. A single spotlight popped on. Cooper and Biggie set a pedestal on the floor in the spotlight, then put a box with ribbons around it on top of the pedestal. They pulled the ribbons and the box opened into a brightly coloured, Troll-sized stage that looked like a calendar with lots of doors to open. It was like the stage back in Troll Village, complete with a tree and a shining sun. A banner with HOLIDAY on it hung at the top. Music played and glitter shot through the air.

"Oooohh," Gristle and Bridget said, impressed. They sat on their thrones, ready for a show. Beneath them, Barnabus snoozed, uninterested.

Poppy stepped onto the stage, having quickly changed into one of Satin and Chenille's sparkly costumes.

"Lady and gentleman, we've travelled all the way from Troll Village to SOLVE YOUR PROBLEM!"

"We have a problem?" Bridget asked, puzzled.

Poppy kept going. "But don't worry, because we have the solution. You guys need a new holiday!"

"Holiday?" Bridget repeated, still confused. "Why do we need a holiday?"

"How else are you gonna buy and give presents and wear awesome costumes and play 'How Many Marshmallows Can You Fit in Your Mouth'?" Poppy asked.

"Wundred and f-f-fventy-two," Cooper managed to say with his mouth stuffed full of marshmallows. One white marshmallow popped out of his nose and fell onto the floor. "Wundred and fventy-one."

"Oh, my goodness," Gristle said. "Excuse me, but have you not been getting our cards?" The king felt that the cards from the Bergens proved they

91

were celebrating lots of holidays.

Poppy and Branch shared an awkward look. They felt that Gristle and Bridget's cards proved they *definitely* needed help with their holidays.

"Uh, yeah," Branch said. "I especially loved the Wednesday one. You know, it really made me appreciate the middle of the week."

"Ugh," Gristle grunted, shaking his head. "Middle of the week." He turned to Bridget. "Told ya, babe."

"Look," Poppy said, "we care about you guys, and we want to make sure you have something to celebrate. And here's the great news: the Trolls have about a kagillion holidays, so you can have one of ours!"

Bridget looked doubtful. But she wanted to be polite to her friend. "That's cool! I guess—"

That was all Poppy needed to hear. "Yeah, it is!"

she shouted. "Let's DO this!"

The little stage was bathed in coloured lights. Loud music played. Satin, Chenille, Biggie and Fuzzbert popped out of the doors on the stage and sang backup harmonies. *"OOOOH-WAH! OOOOH-WAH!"*

"The first holiday we're presenting to you," Poppy announced proudly, "is GLITTERPALOOZA!"

Guy Diamond blasted a cloud of glitter onto the stage. He jumped into the spotlight, his eyes twinkling.

"On Glitterpalooza, everyone throws glitter balls at each other! And everyone gets blasted with glitter!" he exclaimed.

The Trolls threw glitter balls at each other. A glitter cannon went off. *BOOM!*

Unfortunately, the glitter shot into Gristle's face. He coughed and sputtered. *"Aaaccchhh!* There's glitter in my eyes!"

As Bridget helped Gristle brush the glitter from his face, she said, "Maybe that holiday is not really cool for us, Poppy—"

But Poppy, seeing that Glitterpalooza wasn't going over very well, cut her friend off. "Okay!" she said. "Well, if you don't like Glitterpalooza, how about…"

CHAPTER 10

"... **T**ICKLE DAY! Take it away, Biggie!"

The big blue Troll, carrying Mr Dinkles, popped out of one of the doors in the set. Both wore brightly coloured hats with long feathers in them.

"We spend all of Tickle Day giggling and laughing!" Biggie explained. "Because on Tickle Day, guess what happens?"

"You tickle each other with feathers?" Gristle guessed.

"Nope," Biggie said. "On Tickle Day, we all

get tickled by … SPIDERS!"

"Spiders?" Bridget gasped, scrunching up her face.

As the other Trolls acted out the scene with fake spiders on strings, Biggie explained how back in Troll Village, a huge furry spider floats down on a web string from a tree on Tickle Day.

"We tickle the big spider's tummy," he said, "and dozens of little spiders pour out of the big spider's mouth, falling onto the Trolls, who are waiting eagerly below!"

"*Eagerly?*" Gristle said, hardly able to believe what he was hearing.

"Yeah. The little spiders crawl all over the Trolls' bodies, tickling them," Biggie continued as his friends acted it out. "Everyone laughs and laughs, saying, 'It tickles! It tickles!' Their laughter echoes through the forest all day long.

That's our Tickle Day, but it could be YOURS!"

"I'm totally creeped out by this," Gristle whispered to Bridget.

"Bergens aren't really ticklish," Bridget explained, horrified by the thought of a holiday dedicated to having spiders crawl all over them.

But Poppy wasn't fazed. She went right on to the next holiday, cueing the fashion twins. Satin and Chenille popped out of a window on the set to describe ... BUBBLE DAY!

"On Bubble Day, we celebrate with lots of bubbles!" Satin explained, hitting a button. Bubbles started to float up from behind the calendar set.

"And foam!" Chenille said, hitting another button. Foam cascaded into the room.

"And of course it wouldn't be Bubble Day without..." Satin began.

"... LASERS!" Chenille finished, hitting a third button. Coloured lasers lit up the bubbles and foam.

Curious about all the bubbles and foam, Barnabus padded out from underneath the thrones and approached the little stage. A huge bubble formed around the crocodile, lifting him to the ceiling!

"Barnabus!" Gristle cried. "What are you doing up there?"

The bubble floated into a pointy crystal hanging off a chandelier, and – *POP!* – Barnabus fell right into Gristle's lap.

"Oof!" the king grunted.

Foam rose throughout the chamber. Lasers whirled around, lighting up dark corners that hadn't been lit in years. Stringy cobwebs and dusty stretches of woodwork were revealed.

One of the lasers hit Gristle in the eye. Multicoloured foam sprayed everywhere!

"Blech!" Gristle cried. "It stings!"

"Well," Bridget said, trying to look on the bright side. "Maybe it'll help wash out the glitter!" She turned to her Troll friend. "Poppy, these things you're celebrating – bubbles and foam and lasers – don't really seem like Bergen things."

"That's okay!" Poppy called from the front of the little stage. "No problem! We're only halfway through!"

"What?" Gristle said. "You've gotta be kidding me!"

But Poppy was already moving on, encouraging her fellow Trolls to launch into a description of …

BALLOON SQUEAL DAY!

Cooper took the lead on this one, stepping out of a door in the set holding an inflated balloon.

"Yes, for twenty-four straight hours," he said, "you'll hear nothing but the beautiful, majestic squeal of balloons!"

He stretched the rubber mouth of the balloon, letting out just enough air to make a loud squeal.

SQUEEEEEEEEEEAAAL!

One by one, the other Trolls joined Cooper, holding balloons of different colours. And one by one, they stretched out their balloons' rubber mouths, letting out high-pitched squeals.

SQUEEEEEAAL!

Bridget and Gristle cringed.

By the time all the smiling Trolls were making their balloons squeal together, the sound in the chamber was almost deafening!

SQUEEEEEEEEEEEEEEEEEAAAL!

Bridget and Gristle covered their ears. Barnabus hissed and put his claws over his crocodile ears.

(Crocodiles have excellent hearing.)

Branch pulled a finger across his throat, signalling for them to stop making their balloons squeal. The Trolls let go of their balloons, and they shot around the room making rude noises as they deflated. *PBBBBBT!* One landed on Gristle's nose and he flicked it away.

"Hey, everybody," Branch said from the stage. "Why don't we just take a cool five minutes?"

He tried to smile, but once again it came out as an awkward grimace.

Bridget leaned over to Gristle and whispered, "What's happening with his face?"

"I think he's got gas," Gristle whispered back with a knowing nod.

Branch turned to Poppy, pointed at his smile, and whispered, "Not working?"

"Nope," Poppy said. "Still super weird."

Poppy pulled Branch off the stage. The Trolls hurried out of the throne room and into the hallway.

Their holiday presentation was *not* going well.

CHAPTER 11

In the throne room, Chad and Todd used vacuum cleaners and brushes to clean glitter, foam, bubble soap and balloons off Gristle and Bridget. The chamber was a wet, sparkly mess.

"Whew," Gristle said. "Thanks, Todd."

"It's Chad, sir," the guard answered patiently.

"Well, then have Todd clean me," Gristle barked, tired of getting their names wrong.

The two guards switched places so that Todd was cleaning Gristle and Chad was cleaning Bridget. The little handheld vacuum cleaners kept getting clogged with balloons, and the guards had to keep emptying them.

"I don't know about these holidays," Bridget admitted. "They're all for Trolls."

"And they hurt," Gristle said, taking off his crown and shaking it. "I have glitter in places I didn't even know existed. Think you can get your little friend to call off her presentation?"

Bridget shook her head. "I'm trying to stop her, but she won't listen. She's so peppy, that Poppy."

"Well, she's *your* friend," Gristle growled. He liked the Trolls, but this was getting out of hand. "You have to do something!" One of his long ears got sucked into the vacuum cleaner. "Ow, ow, ow, Todd, ow!" he cried.

Out in the hallway, the Trolls were discussing the presentation.

"Okay, first of all," said Satin, "when we sang those harmonies at the beginning, we sounded AMAZING!"

"AMAZING!" Chenille echoed, totally agreeing with her sister.

"Guy, your glitter cannons were wonderful!" Biggie said. "So much glitter!"

"Aw, thanks," Guy said modestly. "The secret is packing in twice the recommended amount of glitter."

"Cooper," Biggie said, "I'm not sure I've ever heard a balloon squeal that loudly! That was AWESOME!" The others agreed.

"Thanks, Biggie," Cooper said. "You did a really good job of describing Tickle Day."

Biggie looked doubtful. "They didn't seem to like it very much."

"But that wasn't *your* fault," Cooper insisted.

"Maybe Bergens just don't like tickles. Or possibly spiders."

While the other Trolls happily jabbered on about how well the presentation was going, Branch took Poppy aside for a serious talk.

"Uh, Poppy," he said, "this whole thing has been great."

Poppy smiled. "Thank you."

"And you're great for doing it."

"Thank you again!"

"But it's a disaster."

"Thank y— Wait, *what*?" Poppy said, confused. She'd thought the presentation had been going really well. Sure, Gristle and Bridget hadn't warmed to any of the holidays they'd presented so far, but it was just a matter of showing them the right holiday. When it came to holidays, everyone had their favourites. That was just natural.

"You know that wise old saying, 'Go big or go home'?" Branch asked. "Maybe we should go—"

"BIGGER!" Poppy cried, cutting him off.

"Okay, that's not what I meant." Branch sighed.

CHAPTER 12

Poppy turned to the other Trolls to pump them up for the second round of their holiday presentation.

"So far today, we have done GREAT! You guys have been ABSOLUTELY AWESOME!"

The Trolls whooped and cheered.

"But when we go back in there, I need you to be EVEN AWESOMER! CAN YOU DO THAT FOR ME? WHAT DO YOU SAY?"

"WE CAN DO IT!" the Trolls cheered. "WE CAN BE EVEN AWESOMER!"

"That's what I'm talking about!" Poppy said,

clapping her hands and smiling. "Cooper, crank up the music! I want it to BLAST!"

"You got it, Pop-Dog!" Cooper said.

"Guy Diamond, did you double-pack your glitter cannons?" Poppy asked.

"Oh, yes, I most certainly did!" Guy Diamond declared.

"Well, now I want you to TRIPLE-pack 'em!" Poppy said, pumping her fist.

"Oh, YEAH!" Guy Diamond agreed, nodding energetically.

"Um, is that safe?" Biggie asked anxiously.

"We'll find out!" Poppy said, laughing.

Fuzzbert tugged on Poppy's sleeve with his hair.

"Yes, Fuzzbert?" she asked.

Fuzzbert let out a string of grunts and mumbles, muffled by the long green hair that covered his body.

Poppy wasn't sure, but he seemed to be asking a question.

"Well, Fuzzbert," she answered, hesitating, "I would say ... DOUBLE IT!"

Fuzzbert seemed satisfied with this answer. He nodded with his whole body and laughed.

"Okay, remember: speed, energy and big smiles! Ready?" Poppy said to her friends. "LET'S TOTALLY DO THIS!"

They burst back into the throne room, running, skipping and dancing across the chamber to their stage, pumping their fists in the air.

Bridget tried to get Poppy's attention. "Um, Poppy, I was wondering if maybe I could talk to you in private for a sec—"

HOOOOOONK! An ear-piercing blast from an air horn cut Bridget off. A loud bass beat kicked in and thundering music started to play. The Trolls loudly sang in harmony, *"HOLIDAY ... PART TWO!"*

Poppy leapt onto the stage. "Welcome back! We hope you enjoyed the first part of our presentation, but that was just for starters! Get ready to sit back, relax and savour the main course, 'cause READY OR NOT, HERE IT COMES!"

Bridget and Gristle sank into their thrones and sighed. Barnabus crawled off to the furthest corner of the hall and covered his ears again.

Guy Diamond jumped to the centre of the stage. "This holiday is one of my favourites, and I've got a feeling it's gonna be one of yours too!"

"Somehow I doubt that," Gristle muttered to Bridget.

"So give it up for Epic Hug Ball Day!" Guy Diamond continued. "The day when Trolls enjoy a GREAT BIG BALL OF HUGS!"

The other Trolls rolled across the stage in a big ball, hugging each other. Guy Diamond jumped on, joining the hug ball. As they rolled offstage, he shouted, "And that's Epic Hug Ball Day!"

Mere seconds after the big ball of hugging Trolls rolled away, Poppy reappeared on the stage.

"Then there's SHOCK A FRIEND DAY!" she announced. "That's the holiday when you rub your feet on a rug…"

"… and TOUCH EVERYONE YOU LOVE!" the other Trolls shouted.

Smidge tossed a small rug onto the stage. She rubbed her feet rapidly back and forth on the rug, then extended her long hair out to touch King Gristle. *ZAP!* A bright spark ignited between her hair and his skin.

"*YEOWTCH!*" Gristle cried, his hair standing on end.

Branch took centre stage and spoke directly to Gristle and Bridget. "There's a very special holiday called SOCK DAY! We spend the whole day celebrating – you guessed it – SOCKS!"

The other Trolls danced onto the stage wearing socks on their feet, hands and heads. They balled up the socks and threw them at each other, laughing. Then they took off all the socks and threw them at Gristle, covering him. He wrinkled his nose, pushing the dirty socks away.

Poppy ran into the spotlight. "You can have a great time on TEAR-AWAY TROUSERS DAY! It's the day when everyone wears tear-away trousers! Show 'em, Biggie!"

Biggie strutted out into the spotlight. Instead of his usual purple shorts, he wore long tartan trousers. He reached down and – *RRRRRRIP!* – tore them off!

Unfortunately, he'd forgotten to put on underwear.

Shocked, Gristle covered Bridget's face. Then his own. (And he'd thought the glitter and bubbles in his eyes were bad!)

Branch jumped in front of Biggie, whose blue skin was blushing red.

"Let me tell you all about GOOD-LUCK TROLL DAY!" he said, shuffling to the side so Biggie could slip backstage and put on his next costume. "Or, in your case, GOOD-LUCK BERGEN DAY! First, you put a shiny pink jewel in your belly button—"

Holding a bazooka over his shoulder, Cooper took careful aim at King Gristle's belly button. *FWOOMP!* He fired and a bright pink gem sailed through the air, landing in Gristle's navel.

"*Ooof!*" Gristle grunted.

"Next," Branch continued, "everybody rubs

that belly jewel for luck!"

Several Trolls ran over to Gristle, climbed up and rubbed the pink jewel lodged in his belly button.

"Rub it! Rub it! Rub it! Rub it!" they chanted as Gristle watched, mystified.

"How is this lucky?" Gristle asked. "Having a bunch of people rub your stomach?"

But the holiday descriptions just kept coming, fast and furious. Poppy and the Trolls described EXPRESS YOURSELF DAY (when Trolls let their opinions fly), KEEP IT TO YOURSELF DAY (when Trolls shut their mouths), MOSH-SHA-SHANA (when Trolls all leap into mosh pits) and FIREWORKS DAY (when Trolls shoot off even more fireworks than they do on all their other holidays). Cooper lit so many fireworks, Todd and Chad were afraid the throne room was on fire. They ran in with a bucket of water and threw it on

Gristle and Bridget. *SPLOOSH!*

The Trolls kept going, energetically presenting holiday after holiday. BLEEPY SOUND DAY, when everyone speaks in bleeps! REFLECTION DAY, to think about what life's really all about! RANDOM TATTOO DAY, which is "not thought out". (The Trolls gave Gristle a tattoo on his lower back that read HUG LIFE.) ST SLAPTRICKS DAY, which celebrates pranks. (To demonstrate this holiday, Fuzzbert slapped King Gristle right in the face with an extendable hand.) FUZZY SWEATER DAY, when everyone wears fuzzy, decorated jumpers. (The Trolls yanked jumpers down over Gristle's and Bridget's heads.)

"STOP!" Bridget finally yelled.

CHAPTER
13

The Trolls froze and everything was silent for a moment.

Shocked at her own outburst, Bridget gasped, "I used my outside voice!"

Poppy looked confused. "Why do you want us to stop, Bridget? Don't you like any of our holidays?"

Bridget gave her head a tiny shake. "Poppy, all this glitter, and the sequins and balloons and tattoos—"

"Don't forget the fuzzy sweaters!" Poppy said brightly.

"How could we?" Gristle wheezed in a tight

voice, choked by his turtleneck sweater.

Bridget took a deep breath. "I guess what I'm saying is none of this really means anything to us."

"Um, okay," Poppy said, not exactly sure what her friend meant. "But I just want you to have something to celebrate."

Bridget looked away. "Uh, Poppy, maybe it's best if you go stand somewhere, like, where we're not."

"Oh, you mean like back here?" Poppy asked, moving to the back of the stage.

Bridget stammered uncomfortably, moving her head in a way that could have been a nod for "yes" or a shake for "no". Poppy couldn't tell. She took a few steps to the right. "Or here?"

"Mm-mmm…" Bridget responded with another confusing head movement.

"Or like right here?" Poppy asked, moving to the left.

"Maybe further?" Bridget said.

"Wait, are you *mad* at me?" Poppy asked.

"No, I'm not mad," Bridget said. "I'm just feeling a feeling that's the opposite of happy."

Offstage, Branch and the other Trolls watched Poppy and Bridget.

"What is happening?" Biggie whispered to Branch.

"I dunno," Branch whispered back. "It's like they're having the nicest fight ever."

Poppy smiled. "Bridge, I think I know what you're trying to say to me."

Bridget looked relieved. "Okay, good, because I really didn't want to have to say it."

"You want me…" Poppy began.

"Mm-hmm," Bridget said encouragingly.

"To step back…"

"Uh-huh…"

"… so we have room…"

"Yes!"

"… to show you more holidays!" Poppy said happily.

Bridget looked shocked. "What? *No!*"

"Like FUZZY LEG-WARMER DAY or CHUG A JUG OF MILK DAY…" Poppy began.

"POPPY, ENOUGH!" Bridget interrupted.

Poppy was stunned by her friend's sudden outburst. What could possibly be wrong?

"You're not listening to me!" Bridget explained.

"I'm sorry," Poppy apologized. "I just want you to be happy. What do you want me to do?"

Bridget looked down at the floor. "I … I think … I think you should leave."

Poppy finally realized what Bridget had been trying to tell her all along.

"Oh," she said. "Okay." Looking hurt and

stunned, she slowly exited the little stage through a door in the set.

Then she ran out of the throne room, down the hall and out of the castle.

CHAPTER
14

That evening, Branch and the other Trolls searched for Poppy in the woods surrounding Bergen Town. They were worried about their beloved queen. Where had she gone?

"Poppy?" Satin and Chenille called. "Poppy!"

"Poppy!" Guy Diamond yelled in his shimmery voice. "Where are you, Poppy?"

Branch noticed a shrub that looked different from all the other bushes around it. It was bright pink.

Just like Poppy's hair.

"Hey, guys," Branch said to the other Trolls softly. "Give me a minute here, will you?"

Nodding, the Trolls stepped back a few paces. Branch approached the pink shrub. "Poppy," he said, "I know you're hiding in your hair."

The pink shrub suddenly turned around and howled, "*OOOH-LOO-LOO-LOO-LOO-LOO!*"

It was a strange pink-haired critter!

"AAAAH!" Branch screamed.

The other Trolls gasped.

"Not Poppy! Not Poppy!" Biggie said, clutching Mr Dinkles protectively.

"Sorry," Branch said, slowly backing away with his palms up. "Wrong hair."

The monster didn't care. *HISSSSS!*

Branch made his way deeper into the woods. Soon he spotted another tuft of pink hair sticking out above the undergrowth.

"Poppy?" Branch asked gently. "Is that you?"

"No," Poppy said in a small voice.

"Come on," Branch urged. "Talk to me."

The pink hair rose and parted, revealing Poppy hiding underneath. She looked sad and defeated. Branch sat next to her.

"I totally blew it with Bridget," Poppy began. "I mean, we've never had a fight before! I'm worried I just lost my best friend for ever. *For ever.*"

Branch took Poppy's hand. "That's not possible," he said. "When you make a friend, it's a friend for life."

Poppy stared at the ground, unconvinced. "I don't know, Branch."

"I do," Branch insisted. "Because *I'm* your friend. And I would do anything to cheer you up." He took a deep breath and started to sing in his high, clear voice, *"Friends are for—"*

Poppy wasn't in the mood for Branch's singing. She cut him off. "Branch, your singing is the last thing I need."

She got up and walked away. But Branch was stubborn. He wasn't going to just give up on his plan to cheer Poppy up. He followed her, still singing about friendship. *"Whenever you need them to be there for you, that's when friends are always there for you! Whooaah, yeah! Whoooaaah, yeah!"*

Poppy wheeled around to face him. "Stop!" she cried. "Which part of not singing did you not understand?"

She turned and stomped off. Branch followed her, still singing. Backup Bugs joined in, providing a steady beat for Branch's song.

Poppy just kept walking, rolling her eyes.

Back in the throne room, King Gristle and Bridget were still cleaning up the mess the Trolls had made during their presentation. Gristle found his keyboard, scorched by the fireworks. He pressed the keys to see if it still worked, but only horrible sounds came out. *SQUORWK! SKWOOCH! BLAIRP!*

"You know what?" he said, annoyed. "No more Trolls in the castle area!"

Bridget walked around the room, picking up balloons, socks, tear-away trousers, sweaters and used fireworks. As a former scullery maid, she knew all about cleaning up messes. She knew she'd need to mop the floor after the rubbish was cleared away. And she was certain they'd be finding glitter for months.

"It's like the Trolls want us to be just like them," Gristle complained. "With their happy energy and glitter and foam and lasers."

Bridget reached the little stage, still set up in the

centre of the room. She bent to touch it and a small spray of glitter shot into the air. *"Holiday…"* she quietly sang to herself.

She stood and turned to her royal boyfriend. "Grissy, maybe we shouldn't have been so hard on Poppy and the other Trolls."

Gristle sneezed. *ACHOO!* Glitter shot out of his nose and mouth, sparkling in the light as it floated to the floor.

"I mean," Bridget continued, "they were just trying to be nice to us."

"Yeah, I guess," Gristle reluctantly agreed. Then something occurred to him. "You know, I can't believe they built a set, knitted us sweaters, took a bus all the way here, hauled these props and fireworks and lights and glitter cannons into the throne room and put on such an elaborate presentation! Just to find a holiday for *us*."

He grunted and shook his head.

Bridget hadn't really thought of it that way. "Yeah," she said. "They did all that. Just to help us."

"I mean, why does she even care so much about what we do?" Gristle asked. Then he noticed something. "There's glitter on the ceiling," he growled. "Who's gonna get up there and clean it? Not me, that's for sure!"

Bridget looked at Poppy's cards lined up on the mantel. Right in the centre was a card with a picture of Bridget and Poppy smiling on it and HAPPY BEST FRIEND DAY!

"You're right," Bridget said. "She does care. A lot."

Staring at the card, Bridget got an idea. "Maybe we do have a reason to celebrate a holiday after all."

She turned to the king. "Grissy, that's it!"

"What?" Gristle asked, confused. "What'd I say? Was it king-ish? Did I sound like a king?"

Bridget smiled. "Yes! It was *super* king-ish! Come on! We have work to do!"

She kissed Gristle and ran out of the room, excited. Grinning, Gristle turned to one of his guards. "You see what I did right there, Chad? That is how a king gets things done!"

"Very impressive, sir," the guard answered. "Also, I'm Todd."

CHAPTER
15

In the forest near Bergen Town, the other Trolls were waiting for Branch and Poppy to finish their private talk. It was getting dark, and the night critters were starting to wake up and call to each other. Biggie looked around nervously.

"Guys?" he said. "Have you noticed that it's getting dark? I think Mr Dinkles is a little bit scared."

"*Zzzzzz.*" Mr Dinkles snored, sleeping on Biggie's shoulder.

"Maybe one of us should go..." Satin began.

"... check to see what Branch and Poppy are

doing," Chenille finished.

"But we don't want to interrupt them," Guy Diamond said. "They're having a private conversation."

"Poppy seemed pretty upset," Smidge said, her deep voice filled with concern.

They all sat in the clearing for a moment, trying to decide what to do. Then they heard something.

"He's singing to her," Cooper said.

"Still?" Biggie asked, hardly able to believe it.

But Cooper was right. Branch was still singing to Poppy, trying to cheer her up with songs about how great friendship is.

"Okay, okay, enough!" Poppy protested. "Branch, I keep telling you to stop, but you keep singing! It's like you're not even listening to—"

She stopped, realizing what she was saying. "Oh, man, that's what I did with Bridget, wasn't it? Just kept going without listening to what she was saying?"

"Whew!" Branch sighed, exhausted. "There it is. I was running out of songs…"

Poppy shook her head, embarrassed. "I got so excited trying to take care of Bridget that I wasn't even listening to her."

She hung her head, bummed out.

Then she heard singing.

"Hey," Poppy said. "That actually sounds pretty nice." She turned to face Branch, but found it wasn't him. The song was coming from Bergen Town.

"Um, that's not me," Branch said.

They saw foam bubbles float up over the hill.

Poppy ran back towards the town, passing right through the group of friends in the clearing. Branch ran close behind her.

"Hey!" Smidge called. "WAIT FOR US!"

The other Trolls jumped to their feet and ran

after Poppy and Branch, heading towards the happy singing in the distance. They soon caught up and all the Trolls ran together in a little pack.

They wound through the streets of Bergen Town, past darkened shops and shuttered houses. Breathing hard, they reached the top of a steep hill and looked down.

They saw something beautiful!

The Bergens had decorated the Troll Tree, hanging colourful bibs on it like ornaments. Around the base of the tree, Bergens ice-skated on a brand-new rink. Nearby, tables had been set up with hot pizza and warm cookies. Chad and Todd were blowing foamy snow over the whole town.

"Hey, everybody! Check this out!" Gristle called, popping into view at the top of the Troll Tree. He plugged in a strand of coloured lights, and the tree lit up. "The tree looks like Troll hair!"

Bridget gazed at the lights. "Grissy! It's so beautiful!"

Gristle looked around and realized how high up he was. "Can someone help me down from here? Chad? Todd?"

Chad helped the king get down.

"Thanks, Chad," Gristle said.

The guard beamed. "You're welcome, Your Majesty! And thank *you*!"

"What for?" Gristle asked, puzzled.

"You got my name right!" Chad answered.

As the king approached the ground, Todd was there to help, too.

"I knew it all along," Gristle said. "I was just messing with you, Chad."

"Todd, sir," said Todd patiently.

The music the Trolls had heard was coming from a small choir of Bergens singing a lovely song about holidays. Bridget was listening to the choir and smiling.

Poppy ran up to her. "Bridget!"

"Poppy!"

"This is amazing!" Poppy exclaimed.

"I'm so glad to see you," Bridget said.

Poppy gave her a big hug. "I'm sorry, Bridget. I wasn't being a good friend. I got so caught up in telling you *what* to celebrate that I didn't even think about *why* you'd *want* to celebrate."

"Oh, it's okay, Poppy," Bridget said. "You actually helped us. We realized that the holidays aren't about all that stuff."

"Right?" Poppy said, excited. "It's not about the glitter or the presents or the decorations – although I do *love* the decorations – but you're right, it's not about that, either. I'm learning as I go."

"Me too," Bridget agreed. "I think the holidays

are about celebrating the awesome things in life. And the super-awesome thing in our lives is our friendship with you guys, the Trolls!"

"A friendship like ours is definitely worth celebrating!" Poppy said, hugging Bridget again.

Poppy looked over at Branch and saw that he was smiling – a real, genuine smile!

"Branch, you're smiling!" she called to him.

"I am?" he said, feeling his face. "I am! Wow! So *this* is what it feels like!"

"You have a very nice smile," Bridget said.

"Thanks!" Branch said, smiling big. "Yeah, this is kind of starting to hurt." He rubbed his chin.

Poppy looked back at the celebration around the Troll Tree. "This is really nice, Bridget."

Just then, Gristle finished adding "Troll" to a banner, so now the whole sign read HAPPY TROLL-A-BRATION!

"Happy Troll-a-bration, everybody!" he called.

"I love it," Poppy said.

"Thanks," Bridget said. "But since we're celebrating our friendship with the Trolls, I think our choir could use some Troll voices. Come on!"

The Trolls joined the choir, and they all sang a bouncy, happy song about celebrating the new holiday together. *"HOLIDAY! CELEBRATE!"*

At the end of the song, the Trolls' watches started to glow. It was Hug Time! As the Trolls and the Bergens hugged each other, the light from the watches shone on the decorated tree. A light snow began to fall and it was beautiful.

Long into the night, under the twinkling stars, everyone celebrated the new Bergen holiday – TROLL-A-BRATION!

And it was totally the best holiday celebration EVER!